# FOR DAD

## 1937-2023

WARNING GRAPHIC CONTENT-
PLEASE NOTE THE FOLLOWING
STORIES CONTAIN: GRAPHIC VI-
SUALS AND WORDING ASSOCIAT-
ED WITH SUICIDE AND MENTAL
ILLNESS.

# INTRODUCTION

Ten One Thousand Word Stories by Alan Thomson

**Alan was born on the Isle of Islay off the west coast of Scotland. He moved to Australia when he was twenty nine.**

He has worked in the Welfare Sector for the past twenty years. Working with the most vulnerable within society.

Alan has developed a writing style that has a raw edge to it and has suffered from depression himself. The Ten One Thousand Word Stories is a small tribute to all who suffer.

Alan remembers when he was seven years old wishing to be a writer. He wrote a few stories, which are long gone from memory except one memory where he got 3rd prize in Grade 6 English. His teacher praised the work, and she felt she was there with the eagle in the way I explained it, along with my commentary and visualisation, was excellent.

Not writing much after that until he was thirty. Alan went back to learn English at a college for adults with literacy difficulties. They printed the first story he wrote in their yearly book. This teacher also `loved how I wrote,' says Alan and was also happy with the way he describes a scene.

Publishing short stories, which you are about to read, has given him a new confidence. He would never make a scholar of literature; however, Alan gets out there and in doing so, hopes to inspire others.

This is the Third Edition with added photography credit and thanks goes to AT-PICZ-Photography for the images supplied.

Alan would like to dedicate this book to his wife and family who have appreciated the struggle with many demons, however, are always there for him.

## Fragile Sanity

He was a very unassuming individual who was now in his mid-fifties, worked in a major bank where he had been since he was twenty. He was married they had one son who was still in school. To the onlooker, he was a gentleman of the highest order, always stood up when a woman entered the room. His manners were impeccable.

He went to his office everyday he was due without fail, never had a sick day, and was a stalwart of the company. He knew deep down he had risen as far as he could go within the bank. Plenty of young bucks who came to make changes, but overall, he was content.

His office was meticulous, in his oak wooden desk displaying nothing except the notebook and pen aligned together in perfect harmony. There was a picture of his wife and son on the wall behind where he sat. Nothing else except the blinds hanging loosely. They only closed for a business deal with customers.

He took the same bus every day to the city; he preferred the bus to the train, even though it took longer, he was happy to ride the bus. His mind would drift too far-flung places, places he had never been. He dreamt of being on a cruise to visit other countries, explore, and adore the locals. The world was a vast place and one day, he would discover it all.

This is how he survived the monotony of everyday living. The routine he endured was all for a goal of being retired, with a nice pension and mortgage free.

He was a good man, did not complain much. He was a very conservative person, believed in being an upstanding citizen, believed the bank would look after him until he retired. He had his future set out for the next five years. Then he would retire with the watch or whatever they would; give him on that day, which was not that far away, considering he had been with the bank for thirty years this December.

Retirement was his dream, first would be a holiday with his wife. They talked about it often. He was his happiest at home with his beautiful wife and son. Even though they did not communicate much, he could not be any more proud.

Once he arrived home after the bus journey and walk. He sipped his 17-Year-Old Bowmore Malt Whisky, which his wife poured for him every evening just before serving him dinner. This was idyllic for him, to be home, being cared for by his adorable wife. The sanity that he kept in check in the outside world was now slipping.

Their house was a period style bungalow which they made home, not overly spacious but somehow they all survived and the garden was immaculate. He was not the gardener; he had a local lad to do the weeding and lawn mowing. The lad attended the garden twice a month. All young-sters needed a guiding hand he felt and, as a true Tory, he felt it was his duty to trickle down the spoils.

He woke at five am every weekday but today was differ-ent, an odd feeling. He could not describe it. He slid his legs from the edge of the bed and placed his hands on his knees. Usually his slippers would be the first to go on, but not today. He managed to plant his feet on the rug. The rapid breathing was becoming more and more. He was about to call his wife, then he thought she would only worry. His wife was down-stairs getting his egg and toast with coffee ready, as she had done since they were first married.

Having never been sick, he did not know what it could be. Slowly, he went to the shower and, as always, lifted his left leg over the bath. In the shower, he put on the cold water first and the shock, which he knew was coming helped shift the feeling, the hot water was now starting to come through, giving a feeling of warmth but no relief from the sensational detection of this reaction.

The hair had to be done a certain way; his torso had to be done a certain way, a regimented person who lived the same way within his own sanity. Carefully placing the toothpaste on the toothbrush, he was concentrating hard, as he needed the exact amount every day. His head moved up to look at his face, a face without recognition. He looked younger, much younger; a boy's face stared back at him.

He screamed for his wife to come, but no one came. He looked around the bathroom. All was still the same. He pulled at his skin and kept returning to the mirror. `No,' he thought, breathing now almost nonexistent, heart palpitating. He cried. He had not cried since he was in school. The fear was taking over. He tried all his tricks to bring him back to the routine, but nothing worked. He hurriedly went out back to the bedroom and his wife. This was not his bedroom; this was a bedroom from the past. He looked at his small legs, naked now with no control; he shouted for his wife again. There was no sound in the cold air.

He did not want this, could not control this, he was always in control. He looked for his clothes but nothing around. He went back to the bathroom and placed the towel around his waist, which was now very skinny, like the small boy that was staring back at him.

He went from the room slowly and moved cautiously towards the lit room. He pushed open the door fully. The room exposed a fragility of the mind. Falling to the floor, he could not believe what he observed. "No," he cried out in sheer angst. His beloved mother's limp torso hanging with the chair overturned.

"Wake up Darling!"

# GOD, DEVIL & I

God shook my hand and introduced the Devil who appeared aloof and nonchalant. The Devil's eyes were wet and runny. Almost as if he was crying. Not the image it has led me to believe through my Protestant upbringing. I will call them both males, as they definitely had the image of males, so no apologies. God was not as I had expected either; he looked dour, miserable and very old, grey long hair with a hunchback and limp. He wore a suit of blue threads with a t-shirt. The Devil was wearing the most ridiculous orange three-piece suit. Hair combed back, looking more suave.

The reason we came together. I was passing a beggar from time to time; I place some coins in their hat. This day the beggar grabbed my arm, and all fell silent. The world was dark and no longer what I knew as life. He insisted that I should meet him and the Devil in an empty bar close by, as they had information for me. I was going crazy, this time! The next thing I knew, the noise of the city flooded back. I hurriedly walked on, looking behind me. I turned to see if anyone was following me, then suddenly I was pulled into a dark room close to the station. Scared, I was petrified!

I gathered my thoughts as the lights went on. They explained why I was here. I am doing this interview with both of them as the world is getting crazier by the day and the whole `religion' thing is basically fucked up, as they both repeated on several occasions.

"We have many religious people pretending to be Christian, Muslim, Buddhist, Hinduism and all the rest," God pointed out. Some are still trying to be true to their beliefs I argued but as the devil said, "I am almost out of a job as those religious freaks are actually more sadistic than I am and they are clever too as they disguise themselves as good religious people but basically don't give a fuck about anyone else. Please don't get me started," he laughed aloud.

"So here we all are! What is going on? Am I truly crazy?" They both smiled.

"Not as crazy as those idiots in charge of countries, nihilistic attitudes and it could all end," God says, and continues. "Well, it is, in a way. No one will listen to the Angels and prophets sent to earth to raise awareness of finding peace within, hence why I came here. It makes me laugh at those pretenders and their bibles preaching from the pulpit, idiots, the lot of them!"

The Devil interjects. "I feel totally useless now, with the way the world is. I cannot get things any more evil than they actually are. The killing of innocent people and children, no one cares! My power comes from leading people astray; some of it is quite amusing. You think I am evil? This is not the case. They nebulously pray for EVIL and hide behind their holy books. We came here today to let you know this and try getting the word out there that you will not survive if you do not stop with the evilness that is blamed upon me. I am happy here and there to push a person into, say, sleeping with a friend's wife or killing someone for an obscure reason, but this mass destruction is abhorrent to me and I am the Devil.

God gave him a look, the Devil retorted, "don't give me that look; you kill as many as I do. Your own supposed son, even though we all know Jesus, was not a virgin birth, idiocy!" The Devil pointed at God, who smiled a listless smile. "You got me there."

God cleared his throat. The Devil is right. You are all stupid if you think you can continue with this bloodshed and evilness, then try to pray all you want. There will be NO SAVIOURS for you, as you are all being ignorant and not stopping this catastrophe. You stand idly by while your news, Facebook, your Social Media outlets are telling you this is happening, but you all choose to be inane and bicker and dwell on your lot, not anyone else's.

The Devil stood behind God and rubbed his hump. "This is what is happening to God. He is carrying the strain of the world upon his shoulders. United in this, it will be the first, and last time as the world is going to end. It is only a matter of time. You think we are immortal, but we are not as you think. How long have we been around God? 3000-5000 years, the planet is millions, possibly billions of years and you pin your hopes on one God? In addition, you love the Devil when you stuff up. A scapegoat, as this was your own evilness."

They stood side by side with tears running down their faces. "You must let the world know we picked you as you are an ordinary man who has done a few wrongs over the years, but you have seriously tried to repent and we have watched your struggle daily. We wanted you, as you are a non-entity. It is over unless people find peace in their hearts and minds. Do not just throw away your recordings of what we have said. You must write it down and you must let people know."

"How can I let people know? Most of my social media friends are not really friends, you know that, right?" "We don't care where you place it, just get it out there. We are God and Devil wanting peace on earth. What's more, you are a person of discretion and integrity." I shied away from this statement. To my horror, I was reluctant to take this on and I stuttered and stammered that it not be done, "as I am merely a man."

"Jesus, Mohammad and Buddha were all mere men, mere mortals."

# THE SCAR

The room was silent apart from the hum of the generators providing the cooling air that found his face. His tie felt tight, and he tried to place a finger round his collar to see if that would loosen it. He was not a nervous man, very calm and astute. He watched the people from the window of the 25th floor; they looked minuscule and wondered if any of them were running to his workshop. Being in this room felt odd to him. He spent many years working with people who seriously needed help. He found out that companies would pay him a fortune to come and talk to staff in the vain hope he could change their attitudes. He knew this would work for a time, but after he left, they would all fall back in their stupid, prissy ways.

He had a talent for bringing the best out in people but also would tear a person to shreds orally should the need arise. His tough upbringing in a remote locale gave him a fearlessness that only a few possess. He surveyed the white walled room, which at best was boring to the eye. He walked to the front table and moved it to the side. He could see they moved the other tables as he requested, doubled and long with 18 chairs. He looked down the middle line; it had to be straight with no gaps.

This was a corporate office where the men will be in suits and the women in suits or dresses with white blouses. Walking to the other end, a young woman came in and offered tea or coffee. He looked at her and thought she must be about 17 and possibly the first week at work by the nervousness exuded.

"No thanks, water is enough for me."

"Would you like anything to eat?" She asks.

"No thank you," was his abrupt reply.

Back at the window, he wondered if he would get through this day, a day he remembered well. He unbuttoned his collar, as he was feeling strangled and suffocated. The thoughts of that winter started to flow like no other time. He was no longer in control. He looked at his Omega '63 watch, he had 15 minutes before the noise would start and the class clown would appear.

He left the room to find the gents, which were close to the room. He splashed water on his face. The mirror reflected back his scar. The reminder of that day remains permanently fixed. He grabs the paper towel to dry off the excess water. One last look, his game face returns.

Two minutes before they arrive, he stretches his arms, takes sharp breaths and he is trying to get back. A thought lingers, though, as it does from time to time. Flashbacks come and go, usually in the stillness of the night, where the shrill screech pierces the air, gasping for breath as water envelopes him. He grabbed at his bedding in fear that would scare the dead.

The suits started to move into the room. They all tried to get the farthest away from him; he was standing near the whiteboard. It amused him how adults can be so childlike when attending a forum or training. He did not smile or acknowledge anyone. Just observed their playful pushing and shoving. He already knew the class clown that would disrupt the class. It was not hard. The noise was almost at fever pitch, giggling in nervous anticipation.

The boss walks in and shakes his hand. Not much niceties, but they knew each other. The boss shouts out to them and demands that they be quiet and on their best behaviour, staring straight at the clown of the class in doing so. He handed over the class for the incoming trainer.

Seventeen people attended. There was one seat available. He sat down and remained silent. The group looked at him, looked at each other. Some sniggered, some moved uneasily. For ten minutes, he sat silent.

Finally, he smiled and broke the silent air by tapping his pen on the table. His voice was controlled and wished them good morning. They nervously replied. He had unsettled them all with the silence.

For human beings, silence is unnerving, but is also essential. He walked to the whiteboard and wrote two words: love and hate. He asked a volunteer to join him and write one word under either love or hate. This went on until all wrote one word. He read it carefully, noticing 16 people wrote under hate and one wrote under love. The reason is interesting that most pick a word relating to hate. An easy identifier, possibly, he thought.

The end of the day was arriving and, as always, he opened up for questions. The usual stupid questions came. When he settled them down one person, the one that placed a word under love, she asked what happened to his face, the scar in particular? He looked at her. Her age is probably mid-twenties. She was intense in her demeanour and most did not talk to her; he noticed.

He swallowed before he answered, "car accident years ago." She was not happy with the answer.

"And?" She insisted.

"A car accident many moons ago. The anniversary was today actually. It was wet. I was speeding. I was angry, upset, pissed off with the world; I lost control and my passenger, my wife, died on impact. After the grief, guilt and time inside, I dedicated my life to change people even if it is only a minor change."

She looked at him, as did the whole room. One wept, all had empathy. She said she was sorry she asked.

"All good he replied, I live it every day, and she is with me every day. Time will not heal, but it will ease the pain. The scar and today's date are my reminders that it takes but a second to change one's life."

## THE OCEAN BREEZE LAPPED HIS SKIN

The ocean breeze lapped his skin. This time he was going to relax even if it killed him. Holiday time was here; he looked at the ocean, the lovely bluish green colour and took a deep sigh. His white skin would turn to a blistering lobster within minutes, should he stand in the sun too long, well a few minutes really.

The sticky sunscreen needs applied liberally, which he was doing as best he could. He squirms as he rubs it on with his latex gloves, avoiding any of the goo going onto him or the sand mixing with it. He could not stand the sticky mess. The feeling on his skin was like the feeling you get when someone walks over your grave. He actually squirms and stops breathing for a few seconds until the feeling subsides. It is the same with shirts and hard collars. Even the thought makes him shiver. He carefully removed the gloves and stuck them in a plastic bag. Placed his hat on his balding head, otherwise the sun will attract to that too like a dog on heat.

He wore an open shirt, 100% cotton; nice and soft, shorts that were loose enough to be comfortable. He lay down under the trees to give him shade and hoped for peace and quiet as he walked about three kilometres along the beach away from the usual suntanned posers, kids and squealing mums that have seen better days.
Looking up at tree branches and onwards to the sky, it looked amazing, and he felt his fragility in that moment. The palm tree taking away the heat, which can be overwhelming in the tropics. Humidity was actually not bad for him, even though he was dripping in sweat most of the time. A tap in the brain turns on as soon as it hits thirty degrees. Listening to the ocean is very tranquil. He thinks back to his youth, frolicking in the water, splashing and laughing. Where did all the fun go, he ponders?

The light was there one-second, even though he was in shade it got very dark. Whack! A ball landed on his face, squashing his sunglasses into his nose. He was not happy, quickly sitting up with the sunglasses askew on his face, busily correcting them. He could see people further down the beach, not too far away, some in concern, and some in hysterics. He growled to himself and mumbled something about kids and them being the biggest pain in the ass.

The ball, luckily, was only a soft beach ball and as he grabbed it, a young lad came running up talking in his own lingo. He assumed it was apologising. He stood up and told the kid, even though he probably does not understand English.

"If this comes near me again, I will burst it."

"Comprendi?" he asks, even though that was probably foreign to the child? The young boy looked at him with his arms outstretched.

"Speak English, sir?"

"Of course," he barked.

The child was about ten, maybe thirteen, he could not tell, as he never had the opportunity to have any of his own. Small, coffee coloured skin, no top, green shorts down to his calves, looked like hand-me-downs. The youngster motioned for the ball.

"Come on, sir, we are all waiting."

He threw the ball in the kid's direction, just missing his head, the kid clever enough to grab it. He ran off with the ball, shouting thanks as he went. Watching him run filled him with nostalgia and some remorse. They all seemed to be fun loving, happy and carefree. He remembers playing soccer and running free in fields of long grass, hiding from the people chasing him.

Oh! How he wondered how he could get it all back? His work consumed him, his career was fascinating, but he never bothered with alcohol, women or men for that matter as they had accused him on several occasions that he was a ` stupid poof' or a `crazy fag,' for being single. That did not bother him, as people were ignorant and stupid as far as he was concerned.

His life was not to have a partner, he felt, as his chosen career was all he needed. Now, though, at this time in life, it would be nice to share his wealth with someone, but as he knew, he was a cantankerous, belligerent fool at times. He must have it his way or people can piss off. Drama Queen, he thought. Now he was ready to find a nice person to live with, possibly too late, he thought. He let out a sigh as his heart felt heavy.

His day now ruined, no longer relaxed. He packed up, getting ready to walk the 3kms back to his rental car. As he was packing all the different items in their specific place in the bag, the boy's voice called him to join the people that were gathered. He ignored it, growled, and kept putting his belongings away. Again, the boy called out. He had heard this place was friendly, but he thought people were being sarcastic to him. This time, he turned to see the boy and several others waving at him to come over. For once in his life he thought, `what the heck?'

He introduced himself to the children and adults that were there. They invited him to have some local food, fresh fish, some rice and some other things he had never seen before. All cooked on an open fire. They tasted lovely and he could not believe what was happening. None of them drank as they were all Muslims, so he felt at ease and did not feel peer pressure to have alcohol. He suddenly felt a feeling he had not felt, gratitude, gratitude for this life given. He looked around at the smiling, welcoming faces. He sighed, and he felt complete again.

# THE DESTROYER

The wind is cooler, with a change in the air. Three days over forty degrees is enough to stifle the life out of anyone. Sitting in his favourite chair, he watches the world go by from his window. He thought how lucky he was to have this room, he can see the cars and the people going back and forth. Most people were locals, and he was starting to recognise them. Today he did notice a person whom he has not seen before, a mysterious-looking character. His binoculars were the small type but powerful. The character was out of place for this neighbourhood. He wrote down the mystery person's movements, height, build, and clothing. They placed something in the mailbox as far as he could see; he could not tell what it was.

His nurse, Jonathan, came in a while later to find him sound asleep, snoring happily and twitching as he dreamed. Jonathan was to wake him, but some days he was rushing and left the old boy to sleep soundly. He will be back later to attend to him. Jonathan looked at the man lying there in his t-shirt and shorts. He noticed a scar he had not seen before. It ran from the left side of his neck for about six inches. Jonathan shivered as he thought about the poor old boy having that done. It was a faint scar. Jonathan tidied the bed and moved out quickly.

Sometime later, he wakes to the sound of a noisy motorbike speeding past. He tried to get up to see it; he lay back down as he felt dizzy. He wondered what had happened to Jonathan. `Bugger is always pissing about,' he thought to himself. After his cooling shower, he went back to the window to see if the mysterious person had re-appeared.

The small area he lived in was very ritualistic and mundane, so a person coming up to where he was and place something in the mailbox was as exciting as it would get for the old boy. He gazed out. There was nothing for him to see. The wind was getting up, and it had a real blow in it. He opened the window to get some air in, felt cooler at last.

He sat back down in his chair that was an old chair. People had tried to remove it and replace it but he would have none of it. His late wife, Grace, bought the chair for him. He loved this chair as it symbolised her memory. She saved hard to get him that chair as he loved reading and she knew he would love it.

Their marriage was not all rosy, they had their vicissitudes like others, but he was away so often, which led to her seeking attention. This was in their younger years when she was a stunning, good-looking woman. He knew what went on and, to a degree; as long as she was home for him after his consignment, it was liveable. He himself was no angel, but somehow it worked for both. The fun began when he retired. They travelled and went out and had a relationship for a lovely five years before she passed away.

Whilst reading, something caught his eye. Getting up slowly, the arthritis was getting the better of him. He peered through the window, but could not see anything. Again, out of the corner of his eye, he could definitely see something move. A dark shadow moved out from the rhododendron bushes. The sun directly behind the figure, it was dark and hauntingly vague, moving fast. He went to secure the patio doors. He was slow, and the shadow so close he could feel the hair on his neck bristle.

He knew who it was now, well, not individually, but he knew who sent the shadow that was coming for him. No training would save him. He was too old, but he knew he still wanted to live. He grabbed the scissors from the medicine cabinet; he dropped them when he heard the bang on the patio door. He turned to see the shadow. He surprisingly thought back to the letter earlier. Now he knew that was a good old-fashioned ruse. "Tricky bugger," he said.

He moved from the bathroom as he thought, `this one's an amateur,' trying to pick the lock, fumbling, `could be a first job,' he thought. Back in his day, he would have been in, completed the `hit', then out within a few minutes before anyone knew. `They send a bloody amateur for me,' he was upset by this as he was a very well-known `go-to' man. Wiithin the Special Services. Typical `pricks.' His mind was racing like it had not done for many years. The amateur gave him time to grab his trusty handgun, which he had hidden from the inquisitive nurses. He moved back to the door as the amateur was finally in. They stopped cold when the nozzle of the Smith & Wesson pointed at their head.

"I think you better leave and tell those pricks to send someone decent. Give me some respect, at least."

She stammered. The amateur talked muffled through a mask.

"Take that off," he demanded.

A young female face was staring at him. About 20, he thought.

She looked at the old man in the eye. Before he could do anything else, he was on the floor, gasping for breath. He could not breathe, gasping hard as lungs started to collapse and his organs shut down, he stared widely up at her.

She bent down and pulled out the almost invisible poison miniature arrow that fired from the glasses she wore. A certain blink and it was on its way.

"Amateur," she scoffed as she carried him back to his chair, closed his eyes, and left the old man. Removing his gun, she would now keep as a souvenir for killing THE Destroyer.

# FATALISTIC ANGER

He shook as the gun started to feel its weight. His skin sweats profusely, dripping from his pores. His mind was racing on a speedway from hell that is his life. `This is it' thinks he! Previous attempts almost completing the ultimate sacrifice. A sacrifice he saw as noble, noble act to prevent any more pain to others he held dear. A pain he caused with all his anger and rage.

He could feel the gun's cold steel against his temple. A temple of destruction, he muses in an already compromised position. The trembling was frighteningly powerful. He lowers his father's pistol and looks at the beauty in the gleam. He wondered bemusedly, if Apple ever invented a gun, how would it look and feel?

His mind churning, writhing with a mixture of hated control. A snake infested pit of evil slithers in and around the receptors awaiting the relief. The pain is so tremendous that the bullet will be a blessing to his contorted brain. The `Black Cloud' that is life; he is finally going to do it after many attempts over the fifty-plus years.

The forced action of lifting the steel to his skin is a way out. A life that he has tried to make better and, to some degree, he has helped many, but it was never enough, always feeling bad that he could not do more. The mess and chaos he caused was a part of a life. Karmic retraction was about to be the cessation plan. The beatings he had and the beatings he handed out. Life is a pain of pain existence, he muses.

The mother of all evils waits for him to pull the trigger, a gun once used to kill other humans on another continent. A gun his father gave to him the day he was on his deathbed. He sat aside his dying father as he spoke to him. His last words were, "please take this gun and get them for this." He looked at his father with bloodied bandages. He took the gun, placed it in his belt, and lifted his lifeless father's body.

He thinks back to that day now, as he will join his father after death. He tries to cry, all to no avail; even the image of his dead father lying in blood is not enough to break his soul. He wondered what had happened to the person who shot his dad. Was he free or dead?

The cremation of his father's body was in the wilds as was his wish. His father was a strong, hard man from a country he did not know much about. He knew his father was involved in crime, as the cops were always visitors.

His father volunteered to go to war; he was the first one at the booth to sign up. He knew little of his father growing up. He was in the Army for ten years from when he was three. There were not many times to remember his father coming home at that time. His life changed that day his father arrived back.

His mother was not there most of the time; he took care of himself for a good part of his childhood. When his father arrived to take over the family, he was aghast at the thought of this intruder in the house. Not long after this, he found his mother dead. People said it was suicide. As young as he was, he had a feeling his father killed her in one of his rages.

From then on, he, his brother, and father moved to another region where they settled and grew as a family in dysfunction as only this family could. He was looking after his father and his brother more and more. The friends of his father were raping him on a regular basis. He never could tell his father, as they were all part of the same gang. The threats of a knife held to his throat, whilst they were atop him, it was a safe bet that they did not discuss this.

The area where they grew up was a violence only experienced by the few in society while the rest of society sleeps soundly in bed. By the time he was fourteen, was drinking regularly. He was nice enough, but if he entered into a raging torrent, then look out, not even his father could dampen that fire. The only thing that his friends noticed would stop him was his dog. The little Jack Russel would move towards him with some trepidation and would get into view, where he would start to calm down almost immediately. The school worked this out with the help of friends, so `Scotty' was allowed to hang around the school grounds.

School left behind him at fifteen years to take care of his brother and father. He worked many jobs all ended badly as he would lose it with a customer, guest or manager. Life was never going to be pretty with this background.

He eventually made some kind of normality, with a family, friends, fleeting friends. The anger he possessed saw to it that not all happiness is bliss. His wife was kind, but what was she to do? She loved him, but she knew this was not going to last, even though he was trying to make it better. Pills, Psych's, Shrinks, wannabe counsellors. How could they possibly help? How could they see his soul? His eyes are not the windows to his soul. They hold a fear not many experience? Childhood innocence, gone at the age of nine, how could they benefit from the already shattered life?

The click decided the fatal death as the hammer fell. The sound that followed pierced the air in a deafening explosion. He never heard anything. He lay on the ground with his eyes open, blood oozing from all crevices of his head.

Peace came to him, a release from his tortured, tormented mind.

# THE CHAMPAGNE LEFTIST

Social media is taking over our lives or is it us who are too stupid to realise what is happening? This thought, amongst others, goes on in his head. Destructive malingering information suckers. His show is almost ready to go. He looks at the Professor sitting not too far away from him. "Nice suit, Prof," he says, smiling in the general direction.

The Floor Manager, who is in charge, demands silence, which silences the studio. Shifting about in his seat, he eventually finds a comfortable spot in the chair.

The Host is a dapper leftist, a champagne liberal who came from wealthy folks but hated the elite. His millions were there for all to see. He tried to use them for good. His family were multi-millionaires. His father had died at forty-nine with a heart attack when he was young. His mum married a rich man from the other side of politics. A charming rogue he was. Taught him about the good in money and showed him the reality of what having no money could do. He taught him who was officially in charge of the world, heads of big business, not the politicians. They are puppets on strings. Politicians and even though his stepfather was one of them, called them all narcissistic, sycophant, socio-paths on the take.

High society hated him as he pointed the finger at them and asked the hard questions. The lower classes also hated him, but somewhere in the middle, they adored him and his show won award after award. To be a guest on his show, you had to receive and invite.

Social Media was the topic with Professor Marcus Elias Stephenson talking on the subject. The Professor wrote a book on Social Media, titled, For the good of the child.

"Ready in 3-2-1."

He burst into his usual wisecracking attitude, a true performer and showman. Making a few comments about the politicians around the world, the usual show that has an egotistical maniac who loves the sound of his own voice. He learnt early on that he had grabbed attention. Introduced the Professor as a clever, wise person, his sarcasm wasn't lost on the Professor.

"Professor, please enlighten us on how you managed to secure funding for this, as it sounds incredulous?"

The Professor was a tall geeky man who obviously looked like he was a brainy bastard. Ginger hair-giving way to a greyish tint. His shoulders rounded and shrugged by years of study and typing up book after book. Thirty-five books in all. The subjects ranged from Financial Institutions to police brutality.

"Well," says the Professor, "it's a very interesting and alluring subject, don't you think?" Eyebrows rose as to promote his speech.

"Ummmm Not really!" He says. "Do you agree, professor that Social Media is for idiots? Like me, don't get me wrong, I use it all the time, but really it is time for some other Mark Zuckenburg to come along and give us some other mind-numbing toy to play with. Social Media is infiltrated by big business now and they use it to their advantage and rightly so, as we are all stupid," he says, smiling in the Professor's direction.

The professor was almost agitated by this questioning style.

"They said you would Grandstand and be obnoxious."

He laughed aloud. "Your financiers, you mean? You do not fool me, Professor. Like here, you write, 'Social Media is a structured and consistent way of helping your children to understand the world around them.' Seriously, you don't believe this, an educated man?"

"I do believe it," says the embarrassed Professor.

"Poppycock Professor! I put it to you that this book is a disgrace and an effrontery for those of us who still feel humanity has something to offer. Did the big Social Media companies pay you, or the advertisers that is Facebook? How much professor did it take you to give in to them? My researchers have found that you owe money in a real estate deal that has fallen through?"

The Professor turned from red to a white-faced terror at this revelation. He loosened his shirt and tie. Drinking his water and shaking.

The rant was relentless. "Social Media is for dumb people who have nothing better to do, models who believe they have fans, actors who think they will make it one day, bored housewives blogging tedious stories on their lives instead of getting a job and a life. Some make it happy to concede that. However, the majority of billions around the world fed false hope and soul-destroying lies by all Social Media. There is no truth nowadays. The story comes from some pimply little kid in his bedroom, fed to a newspaper, and it is the viral story of the year. Then we find out that none of the crap is true in the first place. Nevertheless, sadly, that does not matter. How can we be so dumb to follow the gurus, shamans, revolutionaries, politicians from both left and right, Joe Blow from down the road who does a pissy handstand and 65 million people watch it, seriously?"

"This must be the definition of insanity! We give all our details to them; they supply it to agencies who could supply the various governments. In addition, governments, in my twisted conspiracy theory, mind chipped in to give Silicon Valley money for personal informational exchange. This then creates a system that would collate people's information, then providing it free when requested. Think about it, Census time. People are rightly outraged because the Government asked for a phone number and address. We give this every day to Facebook and others like them. Social Media is corruption of the highest order, but we love it."

"You see, Professor, it is not hard to do, as we only need to research and dig a bit. It cost the studio $100 to get that info on you. How do you feel now about the magnificence of Social Media?".

# VINDICTIVE DESTRUCTION

He looked over his shoulder at the car that almost ran through him. He had to jump to avoid the collision. He could feel the dampness from the puddle slide down his trousers. He followed the car with his gaze to see where it was going; normally he would be running after it. It turned into the shopping centre. His rage was still present, red hot peaking, trying to pull him in the opposite direction rather than follow that unfortunate person. Today was different, smouldering anger gave way to a wry smile in the direction of the car.

His head full of happiness on this day, that person will not spoil it, he professed. His life followed a cyclical occurrence of violence, protection, and revenge. Blackness followed him around like the devil himself. Deep down there was a craving and want for a new life, a life away from the hate and vengeance.

Family was everything. He protected them with his blood and life, if necessary. Loyal to his people, he held close. His father was still in charge, a tough, old style gangster living in a past age that was changing quickly before him. He still called most of the shots but knew he would relinquish control to his son's in the near future. They were more prepared for `the new world.'

The family were all-dysfunctional, his two brothers in jail, father a raging alcoholic, mother not far behind, sister, lady of the night and himself a total adrenaline junkie.

People were afraid of them and their ways. Father undoubtedly mixed up in all things evil, mother, a woman who was very loyal, who turned a blind eye. She was a rogue's wife. Coming from a wealthy family, they disowned her when she married lowly. Alcohol and tranquillisers kept her together. She was neither naïve nor stupid; did she know what was happening?

He was on his way to meet the family at their pub, The Caledonia. His father, who won via poker and gaining a public establishment. Totally fixed, of course, gangsters, never wrong nor beaten. The local heavies would all frequent this pub as they were more than likely banned from the other locals. All were welcome, but if you get out of line, good luck!

Suddenly, he fell to the ground with a thud. The crushing blows to the back of his head, a force that caused his knees to buckle and give way to gravity. On all fours, he could feel the sharp pain from a steel toecap boot that massaged the side of his face. The red, crimson trajectories went metres from him. He attempted to crawl to get distance from his attackers. He tried to get up. Another blow to his face and one to his back gave way to a blackout state.

The YMCrew, neighbourhood young team, found him in the alley later that day. Allies of his, luckily, any other mob would have finished him. His contorted body was bloody and bruised, but he still breathed life. This was a `lesson beating,' they left him breathing.

They took him to the Caledonia, where his mother, who had seen it all before, stitched up any wounds as if he were in the Emergency Room of any hospital. Very handy with her sewing, as her boys were all from time to time cut open. She cared deeply for her family and would do anything for them.

His father was fuming; he ranted and raved, wandering up and down the bar with his baseball bat in hand. He swore profusely, screamed loudly that it unnerved the few brave customers who stayed to assist.

YMCrew swore to help them find the attackers; this was their turf and felt a sense of loyalty. They looked down at him, lying covered in blood. His father commanded that they move and find whoever was responsible and bring them back alive to the Caledonia to deal their fate.

Two Detectives met them at the door. The Detectives tried to push past. They met with such force they decided to retreat on this occasion. They advised that it was not for them justice would be served. Leaving the area the Detectives new, this was not going to be a good night.

Atop the pool table, blood now congealing, his mother managed to control the leaking from his skull. She gave him some Laphroaig Malt Whisky. She patted his hand.

"You will make it, son."
He looked at his mum with his half-closed eyes.

"Mum, I need to tell you something." He strained as his voice cracked.
"Wheeshed boy!" she retorted and placed her soft hand on his mouth.
She got up to leave. He made a grab for her arm, but he was in too much pain.

He woke to the sound of people whispering but could not see anyone. He thought, was this it, hell or heaven? His vision was blurry and watery. He raised his arm to let them know he was awake. His body recovering enough for him to sit up slowly. Dizziness stopped him fast.

He waved for them to come over.

"I need to tell you something," He said dryly.

"I was coming here to tell you about our marriage."

They looked at each other in shock.

"Tae who, boy?" His father knowing very well, whom it is he hinting about.

"You are joking son, no tae that trollop you're nae."

Mother and father both left shaking their heads in disbelief.

He was marrying the daughter of the man who previously owned the Caledonia, the enemy of the family. Was it possible her father could do this? He knew it could be as he had threatened previously, now retaliation would be next.

The smashing crash and loudness of the explosion took them all that day. The Caledonia no longer commands the corner, a faint memory in the old neighbourhood. A skyscraper now stands in the same spot, no recognition of the old Caledonia except for a small plaque, which simply reads Forever My True Love.

# DESTINY VANQUISHED

His walk takes him past the brown murky water of the lake with the trees surrounding him in areas of the park. The birds were quiet today as the rains were coming down heavily. He has walked every day the past three months and largely follows the same trodden path. Today he feels okay but as for yesterday it was black and miserable. `The Black Cloud days,' he called them.

He has been off work for about two months with what the doc called an 'irrational thought process,' basically, depression. His diagnosis took a lifetime of feeling the world could not cope with him and one day he would destroy himself or others. Blackness was everywhere in almost all he had done over his thirty years of life.

The walking was lifting his spirits, but after ten kilometres on occasion, he could not take it anymore and the darkness consumed him. He could never understand why he was like this; his friends disowned him lately as the last attack on his senses left him paranoid, texting people, calling people, and generally being a nonsensical fool. The abuse was torrential with its ferocity. A stalker would have been proud of him since it was that severe.

Over the years, he had reason to be in the black cloud, whether it was the death of his mother at an early age or his teacher being friendly in a most barbaric way. He never knew when the black cloud started following him.

His thoughts today were of a happier nature, even feeling a little glee as he stepped over the puddles. Small smiles lightened his otherwise sullen face. As he walked, something caught his eye in the shrubberies, which led up to the tree line. It was a path, a path he was sure was not there yesterday. Maybe it was, but his mood was very dark and his head would have dropped as he walked.

Not usually one for stopping on his walk, he stopped to look at the mysterious path, which led into the tree line. He searched over both shoulders to see if anyone was around. All clear, he advanced up the path and stopped at the tree line, which the path continued into the forest of blackness. He was too tall to walk on the path; he bent down where his knees started to shake.

The branches grabbed at his jacket, giving out a squealing noise, which added to the intensity of the dark. His phone, he thought. Pulling out the phone, that had a torch, the torch was relatively useless and did not do much except add shadows to the trees that already had him thinking this was a bad idea. Moving slowly as he crouched.

That other noise was very odd. He knew the train line was close and if a train came now, he would be sure to jump out of his skin. The eeriness gave cause for his skin to tighten and quiver.

Twenty meters in and he was shaking badly, he stopped and rested on his knee. He looked back, but it was darkness all around. He could hear his breathing in the cold air exhaling a small mist. He thought about his next move, should he continue or go back? Back to a lighted darkness or stay in real darkness.

The noise suddenly came from beside him; turning to his left, he could see nothing but could feel the presence of someone there, watching him. He was now more concerned and wanted to move back. He tried to turn around. It was no good. The trees had covered the path. The path he could barely make out going forward was a terrifying proposition. Claustrophobia was setting in with fear and panic coming on fast. He started to abuse himself for coming in here, for being stupid, an idiot!

Kneeling, with his hands in front of him, he was down on all fours. Something grabbed at him, then moved back into the darkness quickly. His senses were at the high end of intensity, his body shaking from head to foot. Then again, another grab at his arm once again looking provided no evidence of what it was, or how many was there, more than one, was there anything.

He had hallucinated previously, this time though he felt part of them not removed from them, so this was real to him, very real.

He felt anger now. His anger always landed him in trouble, so he kept a lid on it as much as he could. It was now that his anger was rising from within, an anger that brought tears to his pained eyes. He lay down and shouted loudly, "What do you want?"

Again, another grab, this time he retaliated, grabbing back without success of touching anything. The darkness was pitch black. He closed his eyes, as he could not use them. Inside his head, little lights flickered. Serenity came over him that he had not experienced before. He felt a slight pain, not painful more a piercing of his skin with heat around the area, so much heat.

He tried to move and sit up; sluggishly, he made it onto all fours and moved forward. His side was feeling wet, which was warm. It was raining though. This must be why, he thought to himself. Slowly struggling forward, another grab came at him, this time more ferocious and fierce, knocking him to the ground. He opened his eyes, which revealed a small light ahead of him. That could be the train track. He was thinking. The light was moving. Was this hallucinating? He quizzed himself.

The blackest of all darkness finally came to him that morning. The papers reported that he had cut himself several times. He lay covered in dark red with crimson hues of blood when the gardener found him that morning. He lay face down with wounds in odd places on his body. A thorough investigation yielded no evidence of a knife or any other implement that could have caused such damage.

# LOVE FINDS THEM

The sun was high in the sky, making him squint and wish he wore his sunnies. He carefully crossed the pedestrian crossing. He smiled at the driver and went into the airport. `Right,' he thought, 'where to go?' He looked down at the bouquet of flowers, hoping she would like them. Feeling awkward, as he had never really been a flower man and it was embarrassing, but he wanted a new life and he was willing to challenge his awkwardness.

Her favourite flowers were white lilies, which he got along with some white looking fluffy style flowers and some pink carnations, as it was the only other flower he knew by name. This was his mother's favourite. The florist woman had made a great job. He made a mental note that he would always buy from her in the future. He was pleased with himself, looking at them again as if they would give some kind of reassurance.

The wait was getting mentally longer, and he looked for the Gate number that she had provided. He found the spot. There were so many people at the fenced area. He tried in vain to find a spot for himself. He was not good in crowds. He tried to move his mind to his new love and wondered what she would look like in real life. Would she like me? Would she be as pretty as she was on cam? Was he too ugly for her? This went round and round in his head. Up until this point, their only interaction was on cam.

His nerves now producing sweat beads to appear on his forehead and his shakes started again. His mouth was dry, he swallowed many times to get the saliva glands going. Thoughts upon thoughts, he wished his brain could stop. Telling himself to calm down all will be well. He paced a bit back and forth for a little while and then became self-conscious. He rested his elbows on the barrier separating the travellers from the unruly waiting masses. He wiped his brow with a napkin. He was relieved from the local cafe.

The flight had arrived; his heart started to race itself almost into palpitate. This he knew too well, having suffered from anxiety and depression most of his adult life now nearing fifty, it was not changing anytime soon. His life was full of advice from professionals who attempted to fix him. However, the days all became the same when an anxiety attack happened. If he were lucky, he would have a peaceful day of bliss now and again.

He was getting mad with himself as his flight response was gaining ground on him and his mental anguish was becoming consuming. `Stay he screamed inside his head, you cannot run.' This was going to be a terrific moment in time, and he must pull himself together. He was near a bar, all illuminated as if it was heavenly. `No,' he commanded, this is going to be good for me. This lady is travelling eight hours to see me, least I can do is to be here for her.'

Just then, the doors slid open with a thump in his heart. Out strolled an elderly couple followed by a young couple; his fear was now questioning if he would know her, how would she look, would she like me, on and on it went? The door kept opening and closing, his heart skipping a beat every time it did so. He felt childlike now, looking for her with excitement, butterflies in his stomach. Oh, where is she? Is she coming? Did she get on the plane? She was terrified of flying? Oh dear, is this happening?

The mind went blank and there she was. His heart stopped, not breathing, uncontrollable shaking, staring in disbelief that she was finally here, his faith in humanity restored.

Her smile went from her face to her soul, her eyes looked teary, and the whole area was enlightened as she came through the gate and walked briskly towards him. He moved to the open area and had no sensitivity of anyone else around him, stood there with his flowers held awkwardly towards her. Moving forwards, he was still in disbelief that this was happening. He took a deep breath and smiled, laughed and moved to grab her, all the while trying to protect the flowers. She was his queen; life had given him a second chance at love.

They held each other for what felt like an eternity. Kissing and holding her for the first time in his arms. They could not let go of each other, trying as people bumped them. They moved the trolley and flowers whilst still kissing and blindly fumbling their way to an area almost free from people.

The kiss was so perfect, desirably passionate and sensually conductive, bringing a trigger that hearts yearn for. Their feelings from the camera were nothing to the moment their hearts and soul met. The touch felt their hearts beat, holding hands, holding each other closely.

He felt tears stream down his face, looking at her she was on the same emotive level. He pulled back a bit, wiped her tears, and asked if they were happy tears? She smiled that smile he experienced many times since then.

They gazed into each other's eyes; her beautiful smile was in her eyes too. Her face lit with something, love. Is this love? Are we in love so quickly? He felt love for her; she was perfection beyond his wildest dreams. Looking into her eyes, he felt peace in his soul. How could this be? She grabbed him close, her head buried in his chest, his arms wrapping steadfastly around her. Holding her tight, feeling her warmth, feeling her breath, feeling the emotion of two people finding each other on the internet.

Taking it all in, he cried the tears of joy that his love had found him.

For more Images from
AT-PICZ Photography

www.atpicz.com

The Journey Beginz...

Printed in Great Britain
by Amazon

31306698R00033